Apr 2017

Mother Cary's Butter Knife
Published in Great Britain in 2016
by Graffeg Limited

Written by Nicola Davies
copyright © 2016.
Illustrated by Anja Uhren
copyright © 2016.
Designed and produced by Graffeg
Limited copyright © 2016

Graffeg Limited, 24 Stradey Park
Business Centre, Mwrwg Road,
Llangennech, Llanelli, Carmarthenshire
SA14 8YP Wales UK
Tel 01554 824000 www.graffeg.com

Nicola Davies is hereby identified as the
author of this work in accordance with
section 77 of the Copyrights, Designs
and Patents Act 1988.

A CIP Catalogue record for this book is
available from the British Library.

ISBN 9781910862476

1 2 3 4 5 6 7 8 9

Nicola Davies

Nicola is an award-winning author, whose many books for children include *The Promise* (Green Earth Book Award 2015, CILIP Kate Greenaway Medal Shortlist 2015), *Tiny* (AAAS/Subaru SB&F Prize 2015), *A First Book of Nature*, *Whale Boy* (Blue Peter Book Awards Shortlist 2014), and the Heroes of the Wild series (Portsmouth Book Award 2014).

Nicola's children's books from Graffeg include *Perfect*, the Shadows and Light series, *The Word Bird*, *Animal Surprises* and *Into the Blue*.

Anja Uhren

Anja Uhren is a storyteller – working with images as well as words to deliver narratives. Originally from Germany she now lives and works in the UK as a freelance illustrator, after graduating from the Arts University Bournemouth in summer 2015.

Anja loves drawing, travelling and comics and nothing better than combining all three. On her journeys, big and small, she always carries one or two sketchbooks to record observations and impressions which later inform and inspire her illustration practice.

NICOLA DAVIES
MOTHER CARY'S BUTTER KNIFE

ILLUSTRATIONS ANJA UHREN

for Julia Green and Grimsay
where this story was born

GRAFFEG

A boat is a fragile refuge, little more than a veil of thought, against the cold and anger of the ocean. Who would set out in such a frail construction to try and steal the bounty of the ocean and bring it back to shore? A hero or a dreamer, that's who. A fisherman must be one or other and young Keenan Mowat was a little of both.

He was the youngest and smallest of three brothers by a long fetch. His elder siblings were big men with chests as broad as doors and arms like plaited ropes. But Keenan was too weak to haul a line, too weedy to take the wheel. 'The runt of the litter' folk called him.

His brothers knew better. For all his small stature and lack of brawn, Keenan had a priceless talent: he loved the sea and the sea loved him right back. His brothers knew, with Keenan aboard, they would always come home safe, and with a hold tight with fish.

On the evening when this story starts, the Mowats' fishing boat, *The Mermaid*, rode comfortably on her mooring. Keenan's brothers were in the pub close by taking on hot food and ale to fuel a night's cold fishing. Their chosen inn was old Mother Cary's place, The Butter Knife, named after that prized piece of silver cutlery, and symbol of refinement, kept in a glass case over the bar.

Keenan preferred fresh air to the fug of beer and fry ups, so he sat on the harbour wall outside and watched the sea. The tide sighed and the sea was so glassy calm that the stars admired themselves in its surface. It was time to go. Keenan was just about to step into the pub and give his brothers the nod, when a car drove up the quayside.

It was not a fisherman's car, some rusted old sports job that only started on a Saturday night. No, this was a swanky car, with paint as pale and neat as a scallop shell. A convertible with its top down and all the chrome gleaming. It came, stately as a whale, and drew up right where Keenan sat, with his legs dangling over the water.

Out of the low slung car a tall, ancient man unfurled himself. His eyes were blue-green, like a backlit wave, his face as craggy as the coast, and topped with a tower of foam-white hair. When the man spoke, his voice was as commanding as storm waves breaking in a cave.

"The sea looks fair tonight, does it not?" he said. Keenan opened his mouth to reply but found his own voice entirely missing. The strange man growled on, and raised a warning finger before the boy's wide eyes.

"Looks fair," he said, "but be warned now, Keenan Mowat, that's a sea full of wanting. Many men will go to the bottom tonight, you and your brothers with them, unless you heed me well."

The man's eyes burned blue and his voice rolled so deep Keenan felt as if it rumbled through the stone of the quayside.

"When you go to sea this night," the man said, "take with you a hook, an axe and a silver sword, and be ready."

Keenan nodded again, but that didn't seem to be enough.

"Tell me boy," the man demanded, "what must you take?"

Somewhere, down in his belly, Keenan found a shrivelled shred of voice,

"A hook, an axe and a silver sword," he squeaked.

The old man tipped his head, grimly,

"And do not forget," he said, "be ready!" Then he folded himself back into his car, drove over the quay and into the water without a splash!

Keenan's knees went to jelly. He looked out at the ocean sighing under the starlight. The old man was right, the sea *was* full of wanting. Keenan could feel the lonely heartbreak of it, pulling at him. For the first time in his life, the sea made him afraid.

At that moment Keenan's brothers burst out of the pub, scolding him for not having called them earlier, eager to cast off on such a fine, calm night. No use, Keenan knew, to try and tell them of the warning he'd been given. No use trying to stop them going fishing, when the weather seemed set fair. All he could to was take the advice he'd been given and be ready.

But there was so little time. Already his brothers were on board, clearing gear, starting the engine. In a moment Keenan would be expected to cast off and jump down onto the deck.

Keenan's mind raced through the old man's list, trying to match it up with things he knew were already on the boat.

A hook: plenty of those! Hooks for catching fish, hooks for gaffing them, two or three boat hooks.

An axe: two of those, one lashed to the wheelhouse door to cut fishing gear free in a hurry if it caught in the propellor, another at the bottom of the rear locker.

But a silver sword? Keenan felt in his pocket. He guessed a rusty penknife wouldn't do. His brain rushed through an inventory of every object he knew to be onboard *The Mermaid*. Nothing was in the least bit like a sword made of silver.

And then, an object popped into his head: Mother Cary's pride and joy. It had a blade with two sides, just like a sword, a handle inlaid with twining patterns, and it was real silver. It was small but it would have to do.

Keenan gave the mooring line another turn around the stanchion, yelled to his brothers to wait. He raced through the astonished drinkers and smashed the glass case on the floor. Before Mother Cary could even begin to scream, he was out of the door, down the quay and leaping for the deck with the mooring rope coiled in his hand, and the silver butter knife safe, next to his heart.

Keenan's brothers set a course straight out over the silk-smooth sea.

Further and further from land it took them. The calmness of the sea seemed to have put the two big men into a trance. When Keenan asked where they were going, and when they were going to set their nets, they just smiled and smiled, and kept the boat chugging on.

Keenan stood in the bow, watching the boat's white breast push the water aside, and hearing it sigh in return. Out and out they went until land wasn't even a vague smudge on the horizon. And every time they went to set their nets, the fish moved on, luring the boat further and further from the shore.

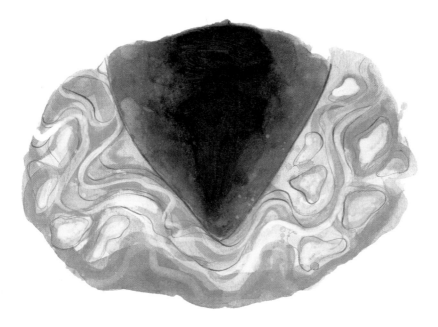

Then, when they were too far out for there to be any hope of running for a safe harbour, the weather changed as sudden as the springing of a trap. Wind howled down from the starry sky and the sea leapt up like dragon's teeth.

In moments, *The Mermaid* was surrounded by waves bigger than any Keenan had ever seen before. They punched the little boat like the fists of a giant, swamping her decks, threatening to break her apart.

And the worst of it was that Keenan's big, brawny brothers stood still and stupid while their boat floundered in deadly peril. So, it was Keenan, the runt, who found the strength to lash his brothers to the mast, so they could not be washed overboard and to wedge a boat hook through the wheel to give him leverage enough to steer.

Keenan fought the storm alone. Waves came cold and heavy as ice, but Keenan wiped the salt water from his face and clamped his shivering body to the wheel again. His boat would not go down!

Then, as if the sea was tired of playing and wanted now to finish this long game, a wave came, twice the size of any that had come before. Keenan saw that there was nothing left to do, but hope the end would be quick.

"Take with you a hook, an axe and a silver sword, and be ready."

The old man's voice rose up in Keenan's heart, and with it a great foam of fury. What good were hooks and axes, a sword of silver against the sea?

He pulled the boat hook from the spokes of the wheel and, with a roar of anger, threw it like a spear into the dark face of the approaching wave.

Like a puppet whose strings are cut, the wave collapsed. *The Mermaid* bobbed, light as a toy on a boating lake. But Keenan had no time to stare in wonder for another wave was coming, a moving cliff of water, approaching fast and purposeful.

Keenan wrenched the axe from behind the wheelhouse door and held its long handle in his two hands. Round and round he spun, building speed and force. The axe flew through the spray and salt, showing its bright steel-shine like a tiny spark against the dark face of the wave. It vanished with a splash too small to see. Instantly the wave was gone, fallen, soggy as a failed cake. Keenan danced, half mad upon the slippery deck, but the sea was not quite done.

The third wave was something beyond all imagination. As if all the water of the deep, below *The Mermaid's* keel, had gathered up and up, to push her down at last. It rose and rose, blotting out the pattern of the stars, until there was nothing left in all the world but one small boat and the wave-mountain, black as rock, bearing down upon her.

Keenan stood amazed, and looked at the deadly wave and saw that it was beautiful! Smooth and lovely, like dark-blown glass. He felt an aching to be engulfed by it, utterly taken and consumed. But his brothers' stunned idleness had gone and they screamed in terror at the sight of this third and greatest danger. Keenan woke from his trance and pulled the silver-sword-butter-knife from where it lay, warmed by his heart, drew back his arm and flung it towards the wave.

It flew like an arrow, small and true, impossibly high, and pierced the shining wave below its crest.

The solid wall of water shivered, sighed and turned to rain, which fell soft as a kiss on Keenan's upturned face.

The storm had passed and the brothers saved, if only they could make it back to shore. But there was water in the engine and the propellor had sheered clean off.

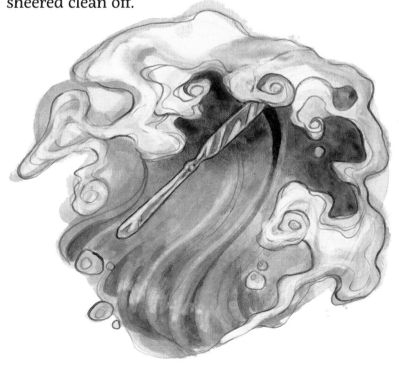

Keenan's brothers, brisk and burly once again, fashioned a sail from an old tarpaulin, and nailed a plank to the broken rudder. They steered the little *Mermaid* through the night, but, as the lights on some unfamiliar shore showed land was near, she began to take on water. They left her drowning on a sandbank and swam for their lives.

The three brothers crawled up the beach as the pearlescent sun crept over the grey horizon. To the right and left along the tideline were bits of boats, and bodies – men and boys Keenan had known all his life. A harvest of ships and manhood taken by the sea. More dead than alive themselves, Keenan and his brothers lay in the marram grass and closed their eyes, in exhausted sleep.

In Keenan's dream, night had come again. A car drove over the sand and pebbles of the dunes. Closer and closer it came until Keenan and his brothers stood blinking in its headlights. A voice came from behind the wheel of the car. The voice of the tall man with the white hair.

"Get in, lads," he commanded and the brothers did as they were told.

Keenan couldn't tell where they drove to, or for how long, but they reached a town, like every town he'd ever been to and yet not like any one of them at all. Men and boys he'd seen washed up, dead as cod, on the beach, walked the streets. Their faces were pale under the streetlights and with every one was a woman – some dusky dark, some fair as spring, some flaming red. All beauties who you'd turn your head to see and not care who saw you looking.

The car drew up before a hotel, lit up from top to bottom like a Christmas tree.

"Out now, boys," the old man said, "time to pay your bills for this night's work." Inside in the bar, they sat round a table, the four of them. Keenan had a drink of whisky, just like his brothers. Then the tall man turned to the eldest brother.

"Up the stairs with you, lad. Into the room to the right. And do what you're told when you get there."

To the next brother he said,

"Up the stairs with you, lad. Into the room to the left. And do what you are told when you get there."

And then he turned to Keenan.

"And you, my fine young lad, go up 'til you can go no further. Then, through the door with you."

Up the stairs they went, with all the hullabaloo of the hotel bar falling away below them. The first brother to the right, the second to the left, leaving Keenan alone on a long, dark staircase. Up and up he went, as if he were climbing to the top of the world from the deepest ocean depths. And there, at last, was a door, a sea-blue door, with flaking paint, faded by salty winds. Keenan turned the handle and stepped through.

It was beach hut! Flooded with summer light and the sound of a soft surf whispering. A girl of about Keenan's age sat looking out at the sea. She was dressed in shorts and an old t-shirt that Keenan thought might once have been his own.

Her bare legs were tanned and her feet pushed into the sand.

Keenan had the strangest feeling that somehow he knew her.

He sat down beside her in the doorway and as she turned towards him smiling, he saw Mother Cary's butter knife buried in her chest, just below her collar bone.

Keenan knew at once he'd put the knife there and was appalled. He started to say that he was sorry, but she only smiled sadly and said,

"It's not your fault, Keenan Mowat. You only did what my father told you. The old rogue wants to keep his daughters forever. But you could take it out for me."

The knife was buried up to its little, patterned hilt. A wound that should surely be fatal. Keenan had heard of people surviving stabbing only to die when the weapon was removed. His hand hesitated and pulled back.

"You won't hurt me," the girl told him gently,

and laid her long fingers on his bare arm. "Just take it out."

Keenan took hold of the knife's hilt and the girl looked into his eyes, as he slowly pulled the knife free.

"Put your hand on the wound," she told him and, as Keenan touched her cool skin, the wound closed beneath his fingers.

The hut began to fade. Keenan could feel that the girl was slipping away, as if the whole world was tilting so as to slide her from him. He wiped the butter knife on his trousers and reached out to hand it to her.

"It's all I have to give you," he said. " Keep it so I'll know you again when we meet." The girl looked at him, slow and solemn, her look as dark as the great wave that had threatened to take *The Mermaid* to the bottom,

"Are you sure?" she said

"Quick," said Keenan, "take it, before I lose you."

Her fingers wrapped around the butter knife, and, at once, green salt water closed over her smile.

Keenan found himself floating down the long staircase with the old man's voice booming around his head.

"Keenan Mowat, you and your brothers must never go to sea again. Do you heed me?"

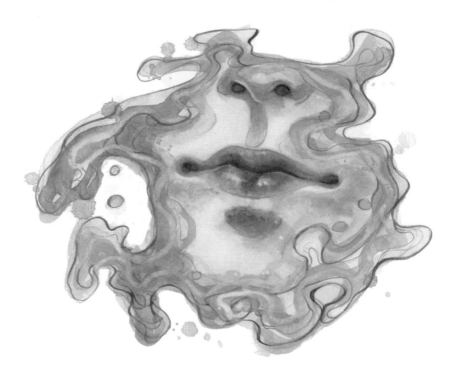

Gulls and crows calling over the corpses brought Keenan and his brothers back to the world. The eldest brother held a boat hook and the other an axe, each cradled in their arms like lovers.

"I dreamt..." the eldest one began.

"I know..." replied the other.

There didn't seem a need for much more talking on that subject.

"Fishing never did make much of a living," said the oldest brother.

"Keenan can go to cousin Andrew in Wisconsin," said the other. "That's a good long way from any sea!"

Keenan Mowat flew to America and, in time, became a doctor. He was good at staying calm when a storm of chaos raged all around him, so he worked in what they call 'the emergency room' over there. His work engulfed him; saving lives, and sometimes losing them, was all his world.

From a hospital, in the middle of a huge continent, the life that he had grown up with seemed as distant as the stars. Only in his dreams did the sea come close, green and cool, whispering up the long, lonely shore of his soul.

And then, his brothers died. Together all their lives, the two shopkeepers – for that's what they'd become – passed within a day of each other. Keenan took a plane to go to their funeral but when he reached the little airport for the hop over the sound to the island, the flight had gone.

"If you hurry," the lady at the tourist booth told him, "you'll get the ferry." Keenan thought, *what harm could come now from going back to sea?*

It was a calm night. So calm the stars admired themselves in the silky sea. Keenan breathed in the cool, salt smell, and felt his heart turn in his chest. He wondered if it might be time for him to retire from being a doctor of emergencies. He went below to his bunk and dreamed of the girl in the beach hut, for the first time in forty years.

Half way between the mainland and the isle the change came, sudden as a sprung trap. Wind screamed down from the starry sky and the sea rose up like the teeth of a dragon. Keenan slept on. By the time the call 'Abandon Ship!' went through the ferry, there was water almost lapping into Dr. Mowat's bunk. In a daze, he climbed out on to the deck in his bare feet. It was chaos. Lifeboats launching, people shouting and the wild sea leaping all around in the howling wind.

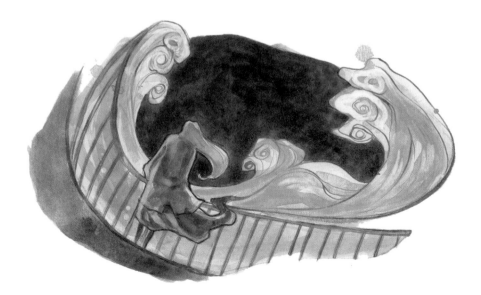

The ferry was going down.

But out in the bow, leaning on the rail as if taking the soft air on a calm evening, was a woman. Her back was to him, yet there was something in her silhouette he knew, and when she turned to him, she said his name.

"Keenan Mowat," she said, "I thought my father told you never to go back to sea again?"

She smiled and laid her long fingers on his arm. He saw, gleaming in the neckline of her coat, Mother Cary's butter knife held on a silver chain.

He smiled and took her hand.

"I've always loved you," he told her.

"And I've always loved you right back," she replied.

The storm leapt and raged, the lifeboats launched but all Keenan felt was the tender caress of the sweet ocean on his lips.